T0398811

Admirals Clu

PEOPLE WHO KEEP US SAFE

Enter here for expedited screening.

TRANSPORTATION SECURITY ADMINISTRATION

Ruth Daly

www.av2books.com

LET'S READ AV² BY WEIGL™
ADDED VALUE • AUDIO VISUAL

Go to **www.av2books.com**, and enter this book's unique code.

BOOK CODE

A V Q 3 5 6 4 6

AV² by Weigl brings you media enhanced books that support active learning.

AV² provides enriched content that supplements and complements this book. Weigl's AV² books strive to create inspired learning and engage young minds in a total learning experience.

Your AV² Media Enhanced books come alive with...

Audio
Listen to sections of the book read aloud.

Video
Watch informative video clips.

Embedded Weblinks
Gain additional information for research.

Try This!
Complete activities and hands-on experiments.

Key Words
Study vocabulary, and complete a matching word activity.

Quizzes
Test your knowledge.

Slide Show
View images and captions, and prepare a presentation.

... and much, much more!

Published by AV² by Weigl
350 5th Avenue, 59th Floor New York, NY 10118
Website: www.av2books.com

Copyright ©2019 AV² by Weigl
All rights reserved. No part of this publication may be reproduced, stored in a retrieval system, or transmitted in any form or by any means, electronic, mechanical, photocopying, recording, or otherwise, without the prior written permission of Weigl Publishers Inc.

Library of Congress Control Number: 2018936772

ISBN 978-1-4896-7624-5 (hardcover)
ISBN 978-1-4896-7625-2 (softcover)
ISBN 978-1-4896-7626-9 (multi-user eBook)

Printed in the United States of America in Brainerd, Minnesota
1 2 3 4 5 6 7 8 9 0   22 21 20 19 18

032018
102517

Project Coordinator: John Willis
Art Director: Ana María Vidal

Every reasonable effort has been made to trace ownership and to obtain permission to reprint copyright material. The publisher would be pleased to have any errors or omissions brought to its attention so that they may be corrected in subsequent printings.

The publisher acknowledges Alamy, Getty Images, iStock, Newscom, and Shutterstock as the primary image suppliers for this title.

TRANSPORTATION SECURITY ADMINISTRATION

CONTENTS

Some people have jobs that help others stay safe.

The transportation security officer works to keep people safe.

Many transportation security officers work at airports. People use airports to travel every day.

A transportation security officer keeps airplanes and airports safe.

8

She helps the people at airports stay safe, too.

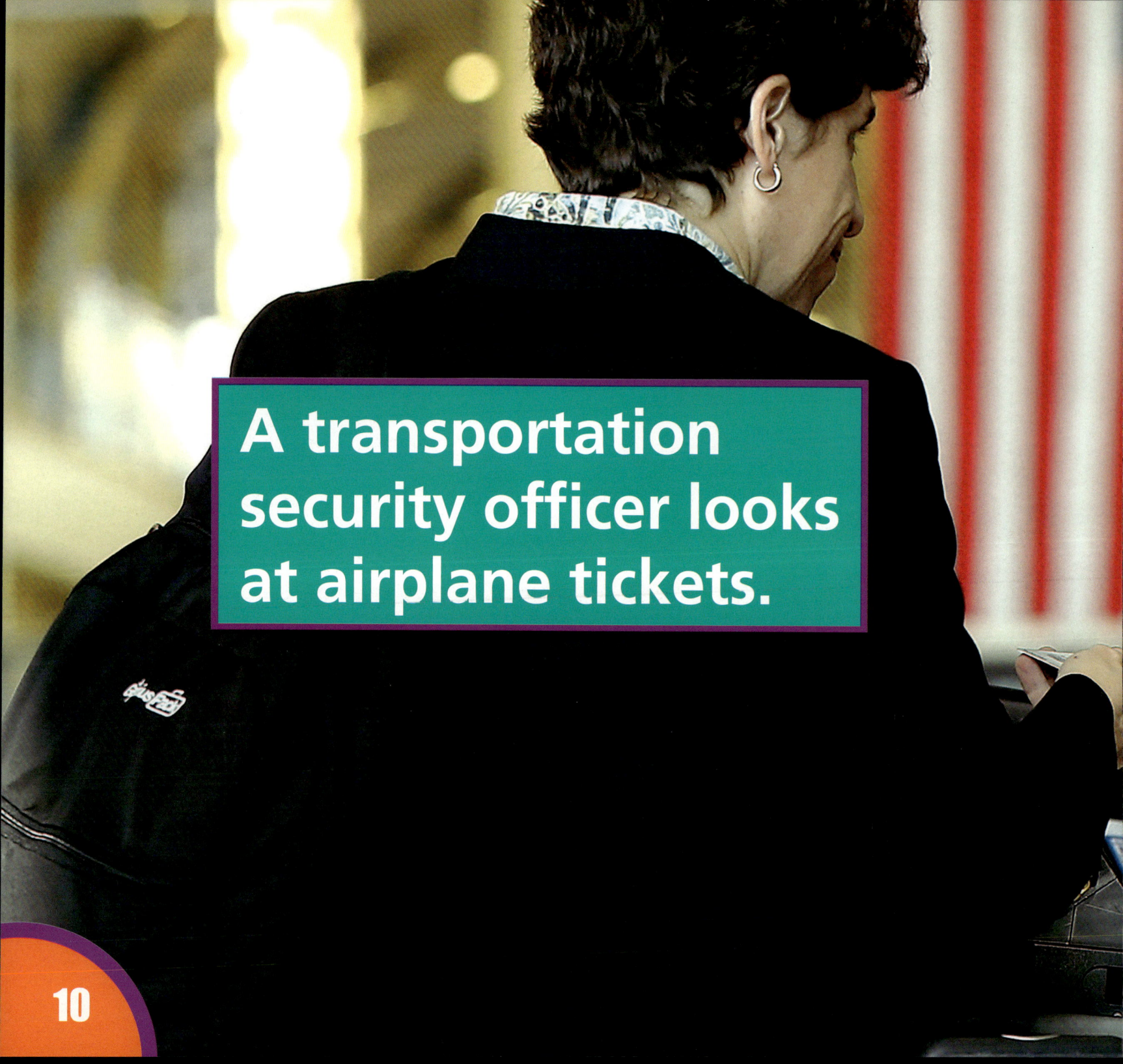

A transportation security officer looks at airplane tickets.

He checks them for names and other important information.

The transportation security officer checks what is inside of suitcases.

12

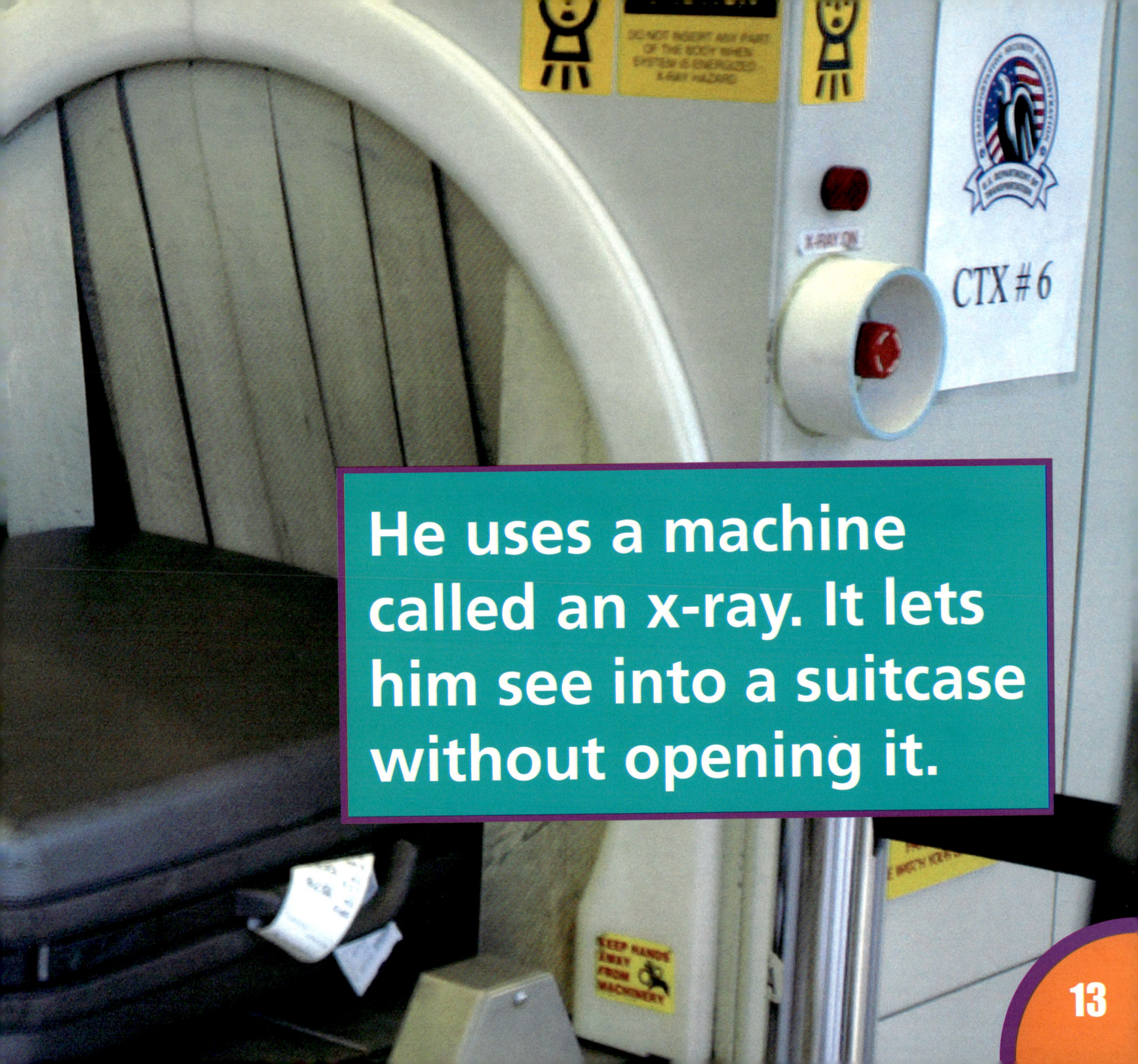

CTX # 6

He uses a machine called an x-ray. It lets him see into a suitcase without opening it.

The transportation security officer sometimes uses a hand wand metal detector.

14

It makes a noise
if there is any metal on
someone's clothes or body.

The transportation security officer must check every bag and backpack.

She will ask to look at phones and electronics, too.

The transportation security officer looks for anything that might be unsafe.

18

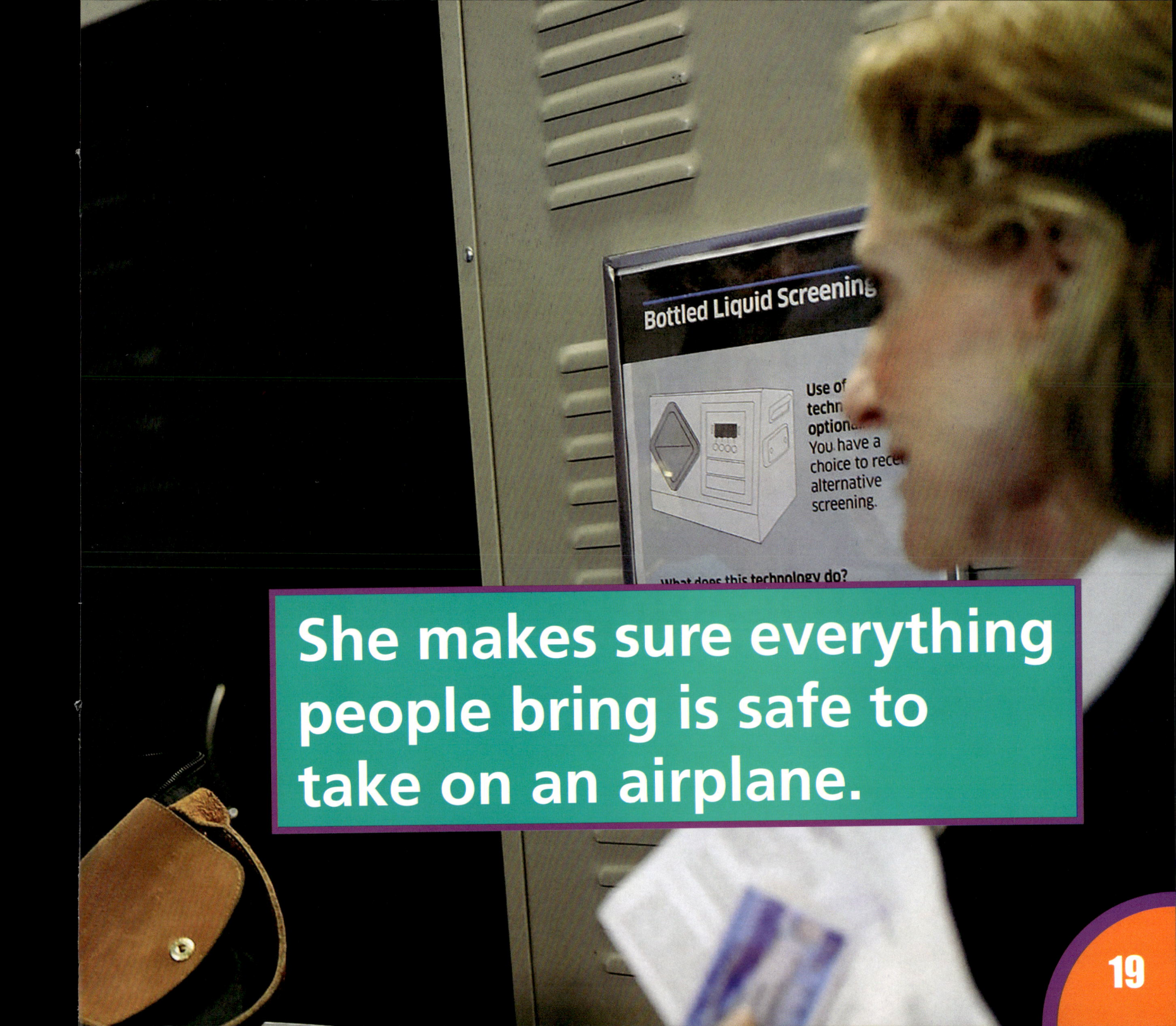

Bottled Liquid Screening

Use of
techn...
optiona...
You have a
choice to rece...
alternative
screening.

What does this technology do?

She makes sure everything people bring is safe to take on an airplane.

Transportation security officers are important because they keep us safe.

See what you have learned about transportation security officers.

Describe what you see in each of the pictures.

23

KEY WORDS

Research has shown that as much as 65 percent of all written material published in English is made up of 300 words. These 300 words cannot be taught using pictures or learned by sounding them out. They must be recognized by sight. This book contains 53 common sight words to help young readers improve their reading fluency and comprehension. This book also teaches young readers several important content words, such as proper nouns. These words are paired with pictures to aid in learning and improve understanding.

Page	Sight Words First Appearance
4	have, help, others, people, some, that
5	keep, the, to, works
7	at, day, every, many, use
8	a, and
9	she, too
10	looks
11	for, he, important, names, them
12	is, of, what
13	an, him, into, it, lets, see, without
14	hand, sometimes
15	any, if, makes, on, or, there
16	must
17	ask, will
18	be, might
19	take
21	are, because, they, us

Page	Content Words First Appearance
4	jobs
5	transportation security officer
7	airports
8	airplanes
10	airplane tickets
11	information
12	suitcases
13	machine, x-ray
14	metal detector
15	body, clothes, metal
16	backpack, bag
17	electronics, phones

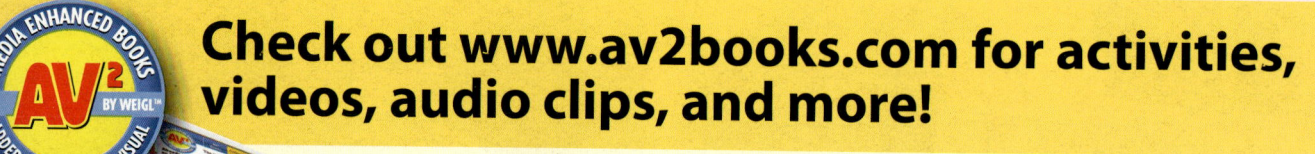

Check out www.av2books.com for activities, videos, audio clips, and more!

 Go to www.av2books.com.

 Enter book code. **A V Q 3 5 6 4 6**

 Fuel your imagination online!

www.av2books.com